My Boston Terrier Adventures

(with Rudy, Riley, and more...)

L. A. Meyer

ISBN 978-1-68197-307-4 (Paperback)
ISBN 978-1-68197-871-0 (Hard Cover)
ISBN 978-1-68197-308-1 (Digital)

Christian Faith Publishing, Inc.
296 Chestnut Street
Meadville, PA 16335
www.christianfaithpublishing.com

Printed in the United States of America

To my beautiful nieces,
Mackenzie and Jordyn. I love
you with all my heart. ♥

Once upon a time,
a young lady received the best
birthday present ever, a new
Boston Terrier puppy,
which she named Rudy.

Rudy was a gentle,
sweet little puppy.

He loved to play with tennis balls and especially loved his football.

His favorite thing to do
when he was scared or nervous
was hold his stuffed football
in his mouth.

9

Rudy also loved playing with his friend, Kazu, another Boston Terrier. Kazu had been rescued by the young lady's friend. Kazu was found on the side of the road with a broken leg. Kazu's new adopted mommy loved him as much as Rudy's mommy loved Rudy.

Rudy had another friend named Romeo. Romeo was a beautiful mixed breed dog. Romeo was Rudy's next-door neighbor. They loved to play and chase each other for hours.

When Rudy was just about one year old, Romeo had to move away to another city with his family.

Rudy became very
sad and lonely; he missed
his friend Romeo.

Rudy's mommy
decided to find him a baby
brother to keep him company.
Along came Riley, another
Boston Terrier puppy.
Rudy and Riley brought much
joy and happiness to
the young lady.

19

Riley loved chasing tennis balls more than Rudy, and he also loved to play with basketballs.

The young lady would take
Rudy and Riley on walks
almost every day.

She would also take
them to the park where they
would run and run and chase
tennis balls and Frisbees
for as long as possible.

One day, it was time
for Rudy to go to doggie heaven.
Although it was very, very
sad, the young lady knew he
would be able to live forever
and never stop playing.

Soon after, Riley became
sick and joined his brother
in doggie heaven.

After some time healing her broken heart, the young lady found a Boston Terrier rescue website.

After looking and looking at all the beautiful rescues, she was matched up with a beautiful little girl named Sassy Pants.

Sassy Pants
(already named) ended up
being just what the young lady
needed to patch her broken
heart. Sassy is amazing.

Riley

Kazu

Rudy

Sassy

About the Author

Photo Credit: RamonaFuhrerPhotography.com [1]

The Author was born and raised in Upstate New York. She relocated to Florida in 2004 and enjoys the outdoors and spending time with family and friends. Her love for Boston Terriers started when she was a young girl. Although she loves most animals and all dogs, she will always rescue Boston Terriers for the rest of her life.

CPSIA information can be obtained
at www.ICGtesting.com
Printed in the USA
BVHW021323170419
545802BV00006B/7/P